Rosie's Baby Tooth

by *Maryann Macdonald* · illustrated by *Melissa Sweet*

ATHENEUM   1991   NEW YORK
COLLIER MACMILLAN CANADA   TORONTO
MAXWELL MACMILLAN INTERNATIONAL PUBLISHING GROUP
New York   Oxford   Singapore   Sydney

For my sister, Ann Ingalls
—M.M.

To Claire
—M.S.

Text copyright © 1991 by Maryann Macdonald
Illustrations copyright © 1991 by Melissa Sweet

Atheneum
Macmillan Publishing Company
866 Third Avenue, New York, NY 10022

Collier Macmillan Canada, Inc.
1200 Eglinton Avenue East, Suite 200
Don Mills, Ontario M3C 3N1

First Edition

Printed in Hong Kong by South China Printing Company (1988) Ltd.

A LUCAS • EVANS BOOK

10 9 8 7 6 5 4 3 2 1

Library of Congress Cataloging-in-Publication Data
Macdonald, Maryann.
  Rosie's Baby Tooth/by Maryann Macdonald; illustrated by Melissa Sweet.—1st ed.   p.   cm.
  "A Lucas-Evans book"—T.p. verso.
  Summary: Rosie loses a tooth and has to be convinced to leave it for the Tooth Fairy.
  ISBN 0-689-31626-7
  [1. Tooth Fairy—Fiction. 2. Teeth—Fiction. 3. Rabbits—Fiction.] I. Sweet, Melissa, ill.
II. Title.
PZ7.M1486Rp 1991 [E]—dc20 90-35923 CIP AC

Rosie's baby tooth was coming out.
Every day she wobbled it,
just for fun.

One day, Rosie was playing dragon
with Sid.
Sid was trying to stab her
with a carrot sword.
Rosie bit the sword . . . hard!

The tooth came out.
"Wow!" said Sid.
"You can put it under your pillow.
The Tooth Fairy will give
you fifty cents!"

Rosie looked at the tooth.
It was white and smooth.
It was her baby tooth.
And now . . . it was out.

Rosie put her finger
in the empty space.
She felt a new tooth
pushing up.
A big tooth.

"I'm not giving my baby tooth
to the Tooth Fairy," said Rosie.
"You have to," said Sid.
"That's the way it's done."

But Rosie did not want to give
her baby tooth away.
Not even for fifty cents.

"Rosie-Posie, you've lost your tooth!"
said Daddy when he saw her.
"What a big rabbit
you are getting to be!"

But Rosie was not sure she wanted
to be a big rabbit.
"Sid says I have to put my tooth
under my pillow for the Tooth Fairy,"
Rosie told Daddy.

"Most rabbits do," said Daddy.
"It is a pretty tooth," said Rosie.

"It is," said Daddy. "Put it away.
Keep it safe until bedtime."

Rosie looked in the mirror.
She smiled.
Then she frowned.
She did not look the same
without her tooth.

She did not want
to lose another tooth.
But she did not know
how to stop.

Fat Mat sat eating a book.
He was working on his baby teeth.
Rosie made a monster face at him.

Fat Mat laughed.
He thought making faces
was a new game.

At bedtime, Daddy said,
"Where is that pretty tooth?"
"It is gone," said Rosie.

"Gone?" said Daddy.
"Yes," said Rosie.
"The Tooth Fairy
won't get this tooth."

"Oh," said Daddy.
"Too bad for the Tooth Fairy.
It was such a pretty tooth."
"She has other ones," said Rosie.
"Not like that," said Daddy.
"No," said Rosie slowly,
"not like that."

Rosie had an idea.
"Let's write the Tooth Fairy
a letter," she said.
"We can tell her
my tooth is gone."

So Daddy helped Rosie write a letter.

Dear Tooth Fairy,

Rosie's tooth is gone.
It was pretty.
She had it ever since
she was a baby.
It came out,
but now it is gone.

Too bad.
ROSIE and Daddy

P.S. Don't be sad.
Maybe someday
Rosie will have a tooth for you.
But not yet.

Rosie put the note
under her pillow.
Then she went to sleep.

In the morning,
Rosie found a letter.

Daddy read it to her at breakfast.

Dear Rosie,
If you find your pretty tooth,
give it to me.
I will put it on a golden chain
for you.
Then you can wear it
around your neck forever.

the Tooth Fairy

P.S. Be happy.
I can wait for more teeth.

"Guess what?" said Rosie.
"I think I know
where the tooth might be."

"You do?" said Daddy.

"Yes," said Rosie.

"I'll go and see if I can find it."

Rosie got the tooth.

"My, my," said Daddy.

"That's it, all right."

"Put it in a safe place," said Rosie.
"And we will leave it for the
Tooth Fairy tonight."

The next morning, Rosie found a
golden chain beside her bed.
Mama helped her put the
chain around her neck.

"What a kind and clever fairy!" said Mama.
"Think so?" said Daddy.
"Yucky guck." said Fat Mat.
He slopped his baby oatmeal in his hair.

But Rosie didn't say anything.
She sat with her family
and was happy—
just as the Tooth Fairy had
told her to be.